The Good Deed Crew and the Aspen Adventure

GRACE NOTES

The Good Deed Crew and the
Aspen Adventure

Kendra Parks

Plucky Unicorn is an imprint of ParksWrites Publishing.
www.parkswrites.com

Cover art by Tom McGrath
ISBN 978-1-952967-00-9

For Ezra and all the new readers of the world

discovering the joy of adventuring

into stories on the page.

Fear not, for I am with you.
Be not dismayed, for I am your God.
I will strengthen you,
Yes, I will help you,
I will uphold you with My righteous right hand.

Isaiah 41:10 (NKJV)

Chapter 1

"How full does this bucket need to be for Grammy E to make a pie?" Jenny asked Addy as she looked at her half-filled bucket of blueberries they had picked from the bushes behind Grammy E's house.

"She said she needs a full bucket," Addy said, plucking several more berries from the bush as she watched her plucky little sister Gabby shove yet another handful of berries into her mouth. Trying to pick berries with her five-year-old sister was proving fairly futile.

"Gabby, you have to stop eating all of the berries," Addy said.

"But why? They're fruit and fruit is good for me. Mom says so," Gabby said, planting her purple-stained hand on her hip.

"True. But too much of anything is rarely a good idea," Jenny replied.

"Gabby, why don't you go and ask Grammy E if you can help her roll out the pie crust in the kitchen while we finish picking," Addy said.

"Mmm. Dough," Gabby said, dropping her bucket in the grass and tearing off for the house.

"Good one, cousin," Jenny said, laughing.

It was the middle of June and the girls were gleaning the blueberry bushes for the early crop of ripe fruit to make a pie with Grammy E. Grace Notes, the traveling string quartet that Jenny and Addy were a part of, was meeting at Grammy E's house that night to practice for an upcoming wedding gig in Aspen. It was also Ty's tenth birthday. Ty played the cello in the group and his favorite food was blueberry pie. The girls wanted to surprise him with a fresh one after rehearsal.

Fifteen minutes later, Jenny and Addy delivered a full bucket to Grammy E in her sunny kitchen with pale yellow walls and baby blue cupboards.

"How are you feeling about the Brahms piece for next week?" Jenny asked Addy while they helped Grammy E assemble the pie.

"Brahms?" Grammy E asked. "I remember listening to a recording of that for the first time as a child. I loved it so much that I pestered my parents to play it every night before bed for at least six months from the record player in the living room."

The girls smiled. They loved when Grammy E told them about her childhood.

Grammy E continued, "I'm sure they were tired of hearing it, but they never let on."

"My favorite composer to fall asleep to is Brahms. Now that I think of it, that's funny because I was reading a book about Brahms this week, and learned that he actually did fall asleep while listening to Lizst play for him," Addy said. "Though it wasn't taken as a compliment."

Grammy E laughed. "I'll look forward to hearing the piece tonight. And if I fall asleep, don't take it personally...the little Evelynn in me might just be lulled to sleep once again."

Grammy E instructed the girls to slice a pretty design into the top of the pie. Jenny made a cello shape and Addy added a few music notes around it. Gabby finished it off by brushing it with milk and sprinkling it with sugar. Grammy E placed the pie in the warm oven and set the timer for 50 minutes.

Chapter 2

Addy giggled as the small paper cup on her violin slid off and fell onto the floor for the third time. Nutmeg the cat had caught on to the action and was playfully batting the cup away from her Aunt Grace who was also her violin teacher. Aunt Grace snatched it back from Nutmeg and placed it back on Addy's violin.

"Now do you see what I was telling you about proper posture?" Aunt Grace asked.

"Yeah, I guess I didn't realize how much I was leaning down while I was playing," Addy admitted.

"It seems to happen more on the newer pieces I have you work on. I think you just get so intent on the music before you that you're more focused on the new notes than holding your violin up like you're supposed to, with your chin and shoulder. The challenge is that it affects your ability to properly shift positions."

"That makes sense," Addy replied.

"I want you to start this piece with the cup balanced on your violin this week to remind you of our conversation. You are doing a wonderful job with Accolay's "Concerto in A Minor". Remember that just a little bit of practice every day really adds up," Aunt Grace said.

Addy nodded and began packing up her violin when she heard Jenny come in.

Jenny had just arrived home with her father from the theater.

"Perfect timing!" Jenny said, dropping her

quilted bag full of her latest costume design sketches by the door and plopping on the couch next to Addy's violin case. "How was your lesson?"

Addy held up the flowered Dixie cup. Jenny laughed.

"She makes me do the same if it makes you feel any better," Jenny whispered. "Do you have time to hang out a little before you go home? I want to show you my latest sewing creation."

"I do. Mom just said to be home for dinner at five," Addy said, peeking at the clock in the music room next to her which read 3:35 p.m.

Chapter 3

It was the weekend before the Roberts' wedding and Grace Notes was packing up the back of Mrs. Gillman's new blue SUV with instruments and overnight bags. The bride-to-be was the daughter of a long-time family friend of Grammy E's, and Grace Notes was playing for the wedding in Aspen, Colorado. Because it was June, there was no school and the group was free to travel and play as their parents' schedules allowed. Addy and Jenny's mothers were both planning to go to the wedding with Grammy E anyways, so they worked out the details with Shaun and Ty's parents who were busy at Yum Yum's, their candy store, that particular weekend.

"And I thought my violin took up extra real estate in our car," Jenny said, as she tried to squeeze her giant sparkling pink duffle bag next to Ty's cello.

"And I thought this was an overnight trip," Ty quipped back, eyeing the size of Jenny's duffle bag.

"Hey, no worries you two. Mom is getting the cargo box for the back of the vehicle," Addy spoke up.

Addy's mom was soon attaching the box to the back of the loaded vehicle. "See, plenty of room, kids!" Mrs. Gilman said.

"Good thing, 'cause Rainbow said she wants to come," Gabby said, appearing in the doorway of the garage wrestling her giant 3-foot-long stuffed unicorn down the steps.

"Now Gabby, we talked about this. We need Rainbow to stay and protect the house while we are gone," Mrs. Gilman said, sighing.

"And Rainbow can't come to the wedding, Gabs. She might get lonely in the hotel room," Addy chimed in.

Gabby continued half-walking, half-tripping to the vehicle with her mega-sized stuffie.

Shaun walked over to Gabby and quietly whispered in her ear. Her eyes suddenly widened and she quickly galloped Rainbow back into the house, appearing moments later wearing a wide grin and winking at Shaun.

"Okay, I don't know what you told her, but thank you, Shaun," Mrs. Gilman said, looking impressed.

"What did you tell her?" Addy whispered after they were packed up and out of her sister's hearing range.

"Oh, just that stuffed animals actually get to come alive when humans are away. She said something to me about a camera and making sure Rainbow had snacks…," Shaun said, shrugging his shoulders. Addy laughed.

"Petunia! It's time to go!" Mrs. Gilman called. They were dropping their snow-white dog off with Jenny's father Mr. Belsky—and also her cat Nutmeg. Petunia and Nutmeg would have some re-acquainting to do, but after a day, they usually stopped chasing one another and became friends.

The dog came running out into the garage and jumped into the SUV. Mrs. Gilman closed the house door and she and Mrs. Belsky strapped into the front seats of the vehicle. Grace Notes put their seatbelts on in the back, and they pulled out into the street with Gabby holding a panting, smiling Petunia in her lap.

Chapter 4

"**A**re you sure this is the right hotel?" Ty asked, as they pulled up to a sign that read *Mountain Palace*. The Palace resembled a rustic cabin and was positioned so that guests had a view of the Rocky Mountains on one side and the beautifully lit city of Aspen on the other.

The inside of the Palace didn't disappoint. Fireplaces with cozy seating arrangements were in every direction.

"Whoa! I could make a lot of s'mores here," Shaun said.

"The decor reminds me of your house, Jenny," Addy added.

"What name is the reservation under?" A woman behind the front desk asked.

The woman's accent reminded Addy of one of those old cowgirl western movies, though she didn't say that out loud.

"Gilman," Addy's mom replied.

As her mom finalized the details, Addy noticed a clear box on the counter with a lot of change and a few dollars inside. There was a picture of a smiling girl next to a golden retriever with the words *Pennies for Sara's Puppy!* Before she could read more, her mom turned around with the room key.

"Let's check out our room, kids," Mrs. Gilman said.

"Can I open the door, please mom, pleeeeee-ase?" Gabby begged, tugging on her mom's shirt.

Mrs. Gilman guided them to the door of

their room and then handed Gabby the room key to swipe through the lock. After several attempts, they walked into their three-room suite, complete with a jacuzzi the size of a small swimming pool. The kids were in their swimming suits and splashing around in no time.

"Hey, what about a hike after breakfast tomorrow?" Mrs. Gilman suggested. She was looking through several brochures of local information left in their room while Mrs. Belsky popped popcorn in the microwave for the kids' bedtime snack.

"Yes!!" was the resounding answer from the chorus splashing in the jacuzzi. After swimming, a snack, and catching the end of a movie about a dog that chased a squirrel onto a spaceship and ended up on the moon, everyone—even spunky little Gabby—was fast asleep.

Chapter 5

At breakfast, Addy was admiring the mountain views through a wall of expansive windowpanes when a familiar voice echoed through the lobby. She took a sip of her raspberry lemon tea and turned to see her mom and aunt standing to hug Mrs. Roberts, a long-time family friend who had asked them to play for her daughter Kara's wedding. Mrs. Roberts was Hope and Grace's godmother growing up and was still a close friend of Grammy E's.

"Isn't the view breathtaking?" Mrs. Roberts commented.

"Absolutely," Mrs. Gilman said.

Mrs. Roberts smiled. "Now be sure to watch for bears on your hike. They can be quite bold in this area. There's even a bear hotline number if you spot one in town. Make lots of noise while you are hiking and you should be fine—just be careful."

"We will," Mrs. Belsky said.

Addy nodded as Mrs. Roberts left. She squinted her eyes out at the mountains once more. "Bears," she whispered, pressing her lips to her warm teacup. Were they really that dangerous? She gulped down the last of her tea as her mind wandered through all the books she had read about bears.

***

The group was soon standing at the beginning of a well-traversed trail-head recommended by the hotel staff. They had been reassured that while bear sightings in town did happen now and then, it was usually related to bears getting into birdfeeders or places smelling of food.

"Is that bear spray, Aunt Grace?" Addy asked Jenny's mom, nodding at the small aerosol can tucked in the side of her backpack.

"Yes. It's from Mrs. Roberts. All this bear talk has me a bit paranoid. I was reading about Aspen and how it is right in the middle of bear country. So to be on the safe side, I'm carrying spray…I'm not interested in being eaten by any ursine inhabitants of these mountains."

Meanwhile Shaun and Ty had found some nearby tree limbs to use as hiking sticks.

"Don't worry about bears," Shaun said, swinging his stick around like a ninja. As he swung it around his back, he accidentally whacked himself in the head.

"Ow!" Shaun said, rubbing his head and turning away, obviously more hurt by embarrassment than the stick.

"Um, we might be in trouble if our defender knocks himself out before defeating the bear," Ty said, laughing.

"Well, Aunt Grace has bear spray so I think I'll stick next to her," Addy said.

The group hiked along for about twenty minutes when they heard the rush of falling water.

"We must be getting closer to the waterfall," Jenny said.

"Yes, the hotel staff said the falls are beautiful and you can even walk behind them if you don't mind getting a bit of a misting," Mrs. Gilman said.

"Cool," Shaun added, as he continued swinging his hiking stick around.

Sure enough, within ten minutes the trees on the left side of the trail thinned out to reveal a rushing waterfall—and a man and a woman about to walk under the falls.

As they hiked a bit closer, someone screamed.

Ty shouted, "Someone's in danger!" but immediately realized it was just the woman upset by the spray of water that doused the top of her head.

"You told me I wouldn't get wet! You lied!" she said hysterically.

The kids all got quiet as the couple continued to spat.

"It's only a little water, honey," the man said.

But as they made their way back to the trail, the kids could tell the woman was seriously upset as she stomped past them with the now red-faced man trailing behind her.

The group looked at each other with eyebrows raised and tried not to laugh, but once the couple was out of earshot, Shaun couldn't help but comment.

"Now Ty-baby, you might not want to go under the falls or that gorgeous hair of yours might get waterlogged," Shaun said in a mocking tone.

Ty took off his hat and whacked Shaun on the head with it. Shaun pretended to fall to the ground in pain, moaning.

Addy, Jenny and Gabby giggled and helped him up.

"Well, hopefully they work things out," Addy said. "I'm not afraid of some water. Mom, do you have your underwater camera with you? I want to try and take a picture through the falls!"

"I was actually thinking the same thing, honey," Mrs. Gilman said, pausing to pull the camera out of her backpack. Just then a rustling and snapping sounded from the woods on the other side of them, opposite of the falls.

"Hey, did you hear that?" Ty asked.

"Hear what?" Gabby asked.

"Shhh," Mrs. Gilman said, holding her finger

up to her lips. They all listened and heard something that sounded like cracking branches.

"Bear!!!!" Shaun yelled at the top of his lungs, and tore off back down the trail. The others dashed away after him.

"Shaun!! Shaun!! Stop running!!" Mrs. Belsky yelled, her bear spray now at the ready in her hand.

Once she caught up to him, she was nearly out of breath.

"First, we don't know that it's a bear," Mrs. Belsky said, panting. "Second, if it IS a bear, the worst thing you can possibly do—is run!!"

"Judging by the fact that there is no bear chasing us at this point," Mrs. Gilman added, looking around as they all slowed down to a walk, "I would guess it was probably just an elk."

After standing still and listening for several minutes, the entire group, even Shaun, returned to the waterfall, making plenty of noise along the way to alert any dangerous wildlife of their presence.

After taking quite a few pictures, the group finished up their hike by skipping smooth rocks across the shallow pool of water behind the falls and watching them disappear into the watery wall before them.

Chapter 6

After their adventurous hike, Grace Notes chose to have lunch at a bistro in downtown Aspen.

As Mrs. Belsky ordered sandwiches, Addy noticed another clear fundraising box half-full of coins and bills. It was exactly like the one on the hotel lobby's front desk. This time she noticed Shaun reading it too.

"Mom, do you have any change?" Addy asked, still eyeing the donation box.

"Um, I think so. Let me check," Mrs. Gilman said, unzipping her purse and digging her hand into it.

"I have some in my purse at home," Gabby said, matter-of-factly. "I have ninety-fourteen dollars."

Shaun and Ty raised their eyebrows at Addy's five-year-old sister.

"Is that so?" Shaun asked.

"Yup. I count it every day to make sure it's all there," she said. Then in a hushed tone, she said, "Rainbow is guarding it while I'm away. You never know when those sneaky leprechauns might come by to take it for their pots of gold."

"Ah. See? It's a good thing you had Rainbow stay home," Shaun said, winking at her. Gabby blinked both eyes in an attempt to wink back, and then quickly turned and walked over to pet a life-sized stuffed bear on display next to the counter.

"Don't let her fool you, she only has 94 cents," Addy whispered to the boys.

Ty burst out laughing. "Ah, that seems more likely for a five-year-old's change purse."

They all scarfed down homemade tomato soup and flavorful grilled cheese sandwiches stuffed with fresh apples and avocados.

On their way out the door, Addy dropped the change from her mom into the fundraiser box, looking into the eyes of the girl in the picture once more. She smiled slightly and closed her eyes briefly, silently praying for this girl who God seemed to be bringing to her attention.

After lunch they returned to the hotel for some rest before the rehearsal at 3 o'clock.

"Mom, is it okay if we explore the hotel a little?" Addy asked after they had sat in their room reading for a bit.

"Sure, honey. I'll come with you," Mrs. Gilman said. "Let me grab my room key."

Addy, Gabby, Ty and Shaun followed Mrs.

Gilman out the door. Mrs. Belsky stayed with Gabby who was napping.

"Thanks, sister," Mrs. Gilman whispered to Mrs. Belsky, before she ducked out the door.

"Anytime," Mrs. Belsky whispered back before the door clicked closed.

"So where is the real pool?" Shaun asked. "I mean, we pretty much have one in our room, but isn't there a real one somewhere?"

"I saw a sign for it near the lobby when we had breakfast this morning," Jenny said.

They stepped from the elevator into the lobby and were pleasantly surprised to see the bride and groom-to-be near the front sliding doors. Kara spotted them and smiled wide.

"Hello there Grace Notes! We are so excited to have you play for our special day!" she said.

"Thank you. We look forward to playing," Shaun said, returning her smile.

"Are you going to the rehearsal now?" Mrs. Gilman asked.

"Can you tell?" Kara asked, laughing as her fiancé and groom-to-be peered to the side of an armload of boxes full of decorations. He attempted a nod of hello and about dropped them.

"Can I help you carry those?" Ty asked, reaching up and grabbing the top box.

"Sure, thanks," Blake said, his look of surprise now visible with one less box on the stack.

"Our car is just outside the door," Kara said.

"I'll just follow you then," Ty said, smiling.

Mrs. Gillman watched them load the car.

"We'll see you at 3 o'clock," Mrs. Gilman called out, waving as Ty slipped back in through the sliding door.

"Ty, that was so kind of you to help without being asked. I'm impressed," Mrs. Gilman said.

Ty shrugged his shoulders. "My dad always

says it's more fun to help than to stand by and watch."

Chapter 7

Two hours later, Grace Notes arrived at Sunset Ranch for the wedding rehearsal. Several women were tying silk blue ribbons around bouquets of flowers at the end of rows of white chairs. The chairs were set up facing a turquoise-blue lake that sparkled in the sunlight. Beyond the lake was a breathtaking view of the Maroon Bell mountains. Jenny and Addy gasped aloud.

"I am so getting married here someday," Jenny whispered.

"Me too," Addy whispered back.

A decorative white tent with several roofed peaks was set up to the right of the space reserved for the wedding ceremony. People were bustling around placing dance floor tiles down and setting up round tables for the next day's wedding.

The young musicians were walking toward the white chairs next to the lake when they heard someone yell, "Look out! Horse on the loose!"

They heard hooves galloping closer but didn't see a horse. Suddenly a boy with a cowboy hat on came sprinting through the tent in their direction, knocking over several pots of lilies on his way. He pushed between Addy and Ty, causing Addy to fall on her fanny.

"Ow!" she yelped.

"Sorry!" he yelled over his shoulder.

Ty ran over and helped Addy back to her feet.

The galloping sound rose in a steep crescendo and a chestnut brown horse with one white leg appeared around the corner of the tent.

"Whoa, Rocket! Whoa!" the boy shouted, skidding to a stop about twenty feet before the horse. He held up his hands as if putting up a force field, and the horses' gallop slowed to a prance.

"That's right, steady now," the boy said, slowly reaching out and grasping the reins attached to the horses' bridle.

The horse snorted and shook its head a few times, still pawing at the ground. The young cowboy gently patted the white blaze on its nose and whispered quietly to it. It took one last deep breath and let out a whinny. The boy laughed.

"That's my Rocket," he said. "All I have to do is mention a carrot and I'm your best friend again."

Seeing that the horse was calmed, the boy turned back to Addy and flashed a broad smile. She guessed that the boy was about her age.

"I am so sorry about that," the boy said. "Are

you okay?"

"Um, yeah. Just a little startled is all," Addy replied.

"As was this guy," the boy said, nodding to the horse. "We were working on some lead training when he got spooked."

"Sorry, I'm Sam by the way," he added, transferring the reins to his left hand and offering Addy his right hand.

"I'm Addy. It's nice to meet you," she said.

Before they could speak more, a woman with gorgeous jet-black curly hair appeared. She was wearing a cowgirl hat and had a large turquoise belt buckle, the same shade as the nearby lake.

"Sam! What is Rocket doing over here?" she asked in an alarmed tone.

"Mom, I'm so sorry. He got spooked. I think it was a—"

But before he could finish his sentence, his

mom interrupted his explanation with a stern look.

"We'll talk about it more back at the barn, buddy. Why don't you take Rocket there now."

"Yes, Mom," Sam said, turning back to the group. "It was nice meeting y'all," he said, tipping his hat at them as he lead Rocket away.

"Are you kids alright?" the woman asked. "I'm so sorry about this."

"No harm done," Addy said.

"Other than some dust on your fanny, Cuz," Jenny whispered to her, giggling.

Addy's face turned bright red and she elbowed Jenny in the side.

Mrs. Roberts arrived and spoke for a moment with the woman.

Then Mrs. Roberts turned to them and said, "We have stands and chairs set up for you over here."

She walked them over to the front corner of the outdoor ceremony area where they immediately noticed white envelopes on their music stands. Upon closer inspection, they saw each of their names written on them in calligraphy. As soon as she left, they opened them up and looked at one another with wide eyes.

"Two hundred dollars?! I'm rich!" Jenny whisper-squealed to Addy.

"Me too!" Addy whispered back, her eyes wide.

Ty and Shaun opened their envelopes and looked up with surprised smiles.

"Alright! Now we can get those new titanium biking sunglasses!" Shaun said to Ty, who gave him a high five.

They pulled out their instruments and began tuning them. The wedding rehearsal started in twenty minutes.

"Let's play through Vivaldi's "Spring" to warm up," Jenny suggested.

"Great suggestion," Addy said, rifling through her music to find it. "Oh, I forgot to tape this one. Does anyone have any clear tape?"

"I do," Jenny said, getting up to pull some out of her quilted violin case. "I just left a roll in my case because I never used to have it when I needed it at the last minute. Scotch tape, lip gloss, and mints are my stocked items in my case these days."

Addy laughed. "Good idea and thank you! There isn't a good place to turn a page on this one."

Addy laid out several pages of music and taped them together.

The group finished their piece and then listened to the older pastor who had arrived. He was giving instructions to the wedding party now congregated in front of the chairs.

"Blake, you and your groomsmen will be standing here and waiting on the ladies to come on down the aisle. Ladies, you will be walking down the aisle from behind the chairs back there," the pastor said, pointing to the back row of chairs.

Turning to Grace Notes, he said, "Can you play a bit of what the ladies will walk down the aisle to, so they know what to listen for?"

"Sure thing," Shaun answered, and Addy and Ty started playing Pachabel's "Kanon in D".

"Thank you," he nodded to them. "And remember, bridesmaids, that this is not a race. Each of you must wait for the person in front of you to walk to the front of the aisle before you begin moving down the aisle. Once your flower girl arrives up here, everyone will stand and turn around…Grace Notes, would you play what Kara needs to listen for before she begins her walk into Blake's arms here?"

Ty nodded and played the famous bridal processional intro, "dah-da-da-dah-dah-daah-daah" on his cello.

"And then it's 'Here Comes the Bride,' am I

correct?" the pastor asked.

Ty nodded.

The pastor talked through the details of the rest of the ceremony, and, after a practice of the processional and recessional, he dismissed them by offering a prayer over them all.

Kara and Blake approached them afterwards and invited them to the rehearsal dinner being held at a nearby restaurant.

"Great job, kids," Mrs. Belsky said, as they waved good-bye to Kara and Blake. "I am so proud of you all. You are going to make their day so special tomorrow."

Chapter 8

Saturday morning was full of swimming which meant Grace Notes was hungry for an early lunch. Another hotel guest, whose kids had also been swimming all morning, suggested they try the Sleepy Bear Grill downtown. Known for its kid-friendly menu, the restaurant had individual pizzas kids could assemble on their own and then receive back freshly warmed from the grill.

"Mmmm. This place smells awesome," Shaun said, patting his stomach. They had just climbed the front steps and walked in the door of the Sleepy Bear

Grill.

The group sat together at a table overlooking the mountains beyond the parking lot. A chipper waitress greeted them and then set a warm basket of bear-shaped bread on the table before them.

"Oh, that's so cute," Jenny said.

"Seriously. How are you supposed to eat a cute teddy bear?" Addy asked.

"Mmmm. I for one have no problem eating a bear," Shaun said, licking his lips.

"Mmmm. Buttered bear," Ty said.

Gabby glared at the boys and instinctively pulled the bear bread in front of her and wrapped her arms around the basket for protection.

"That's right, Gabs. Protect our little bear," Addy said.

"Aww, come on!" Shaun exclaimed.

"We're starving!" Ty added.

Jenny laughed, but Gabby stayed silent. She

was torn between saving the bear and saving the boys from hunger.

The waitress appeared and took their orders. She also solved the bear bread issue by promising to bring more bread back along with their drink order.

"We have two hours until we need to leave for the wedding. So that means we probably need to start getting ready once we return to the hotel," Mrs. Gilman said, looking down at her phone.

"Well, the instruments are already loaded in the vehicle, so that should save us some time too," Mrs. Belsky added.

The waitress returned with their drinks and brought their pizza crusts and toppings for them to assemble their own personal pizzas.

"This is so fun!" Gabby said, grabbing a heaping spoonful of sauce and swirling it around her crust.

"Yeah, I'm going to make mine a super supreme," Shaun said, piling his sky high with toppings.

"I'm going with the meat special," Ty said, loading pepperoni, sausage and bacon on his.

"Mmmm. I just want cheese. I looooove cheese," Addy said, carefully arranging her cheese to the very edges of her pizza.

Jenny was artfully placing veggies around her pizza into a mosaic.

"Okay, I'm impressed," Shaun said, watching Jenny. "Are you going to be able to eat that?" he asked.

"What do you mean?" Jenny asked.

"It's too pretty to eat," Addy said. "Right, Shaun?"

"Yeah, I mean it looks just like a Tiffany stained glass window of colored vegetable glass," he said, gesturing towards the window.

As he glanced at the window, Shaun leapt up

on the booth seat to look more closely out the window.

"Oooooooh no. That's not good," was all he could say before Mrs. Belsky started yelling, "Bear! There's a bear! Bear! Bear!!"

Mrs. Gilman pushed herself over to the window and her voice pitched up as she screamed, "It's heading towards my vehicle!!"

The next thing they knew, the giant black bear was climbing up on top of their vehicle. They were all making such a commotion at this point that their server and the restaurant manager rushed over.

"There is a bear on our vehicle!" Mrs. Gilman yelled.

"Well, Ma'am, I'm sorry about this. It does happen every now and then. I do apologize," the manager said.

The bear climbed over the front of the vehicle. They all sighed with relief…until they realized it wasn't going anywhere. They watched as it continued to lumber around the vehicle.

"Will it leave soon? Should we make some noise or something to shoo it away?" Mrs. Belsky asked the manager.

"Um, I think we have a bigger problem, people," Shaun said. As they were discussing what to do, the bear actually began trying to open the doors of the vehicle.

"Hope, are the doors locked?" Mrs. Belsky screamed.

"Oh my gosh! I don't remember. I think so. Let me find my keys!" Mrs. Gilman said, fumbling with her purse and then rifling through it for her keys. "Oh no! Mommy, you can never find your keys, and now the bear's gonna drive away in our car!" Gabby said, beginning to cry.

"Gabs, stay calm. Mom, check the outside pocket," Addy said, trying to help.

Mrs. Gilman found her keys and hit the lock button, but not in time. The bear had managed to open one of the back doors and began pawing around inside.

"I'm calling the park rangers. They are always close by and deal with bears a lot around town," the manager said, punching buttons on his phone and holding his forehead in concentration. "I am so sorry about this!"

"Do you have any food or anything in your vehicle, Ma'am?" the waitress asked.

"Just some crackers, I think," Mrs. Gilman said, her hand on her head trying to remember. "What kind of wild animal knows how to open car doors? This is nuts!!"

"What if it gets our instruments?" Ty asked, now clearly concerned.

As if on cue, the bear suddenly pulled its head back out of the vehicle with the bag of crackers and

Jenny's quilted violin case in its paws.

"Nooooooooooo!!!!!!!!!!!!!" Jenny screamed, jumping onto the table and pounding on the window. "That's my violin!!!!!! I need it to play tomorrow!!!! And I spent days making that new case!! We have to do something!!!!!"

The manager wasn't kidding about the speed of the rangers in their response, as the ranger's truck pulled into the parking lot.

Meanwhile, Shaun grabbed Mrs. Gilman's keys and, with a look of confident determination, pointed them at the window and hit the red alarm button. The vehicle alarm and the blaring sirens from the ranger's truck were enough for the bear to become startled, drop the violin case and lumber off back into the woods, the cracker bag tightly clutched in its clawed hand.

"Wooooo-hooooo! You did it, brother!!!!" Ty said, high-fiving Shaun for his quick thinking.

"Oh my gosh, I have to see if my violin is alright!" Jenny yelled, scrambling off the table.

"Hold on, honey! We have to make sure it's safe!" Mrs. Belsky said, clutching her daughter's arm. After quickly surveying the scene, she stood up and ran with Jenny to the door and down the steps. They ran to the parking lot behind the restaurant.

Mrs. Belsky waved to the ranger, who motioned that it was safe, and Jenny quickly determined that the case had done its job to protect her instrument. The violin had survived the fall.

Jenny turned to give a thumbs up to the others, but found her friends standing right behind her.

"Next time you really need to make sure you lock your doors, Ma'am," the ranger said before he drove off.

"So much for carrying lip gloss and mints in my case!" Jenny said to her mother, shaking her head.

"And so much for the Sleepy Bear Grill!" Ty said.

"Yeah, more like the Sneaky Bear Grill!" Shaun quipped.

Addy and her mother held a sobbing Gabby who was sad that the bear had eaten her bag of fish-shaped crackers.

Chapter 9

It was 2:15 p.m. and Grace Notes had just finished tuning up their instruments and arranging their music for the wedding.

"Let's take a final stretch break and then meet back here in ten minutes to begin the pre-wedding music," Addy suggested.

"Sounds good," Ty and Shaun agreed in unison.

"Perfect," Jenny said. "I think I might have just seen Grammy E with my mom. I'm going to go find them."

Addy began walking to where her mom and Gabby were sitting at a table in the reception tent. On her way, she saw Sam, the boy with the cowboy hat they had met the previous night, leading a white horse over to a barn in the distance. She watched where he was walking from and spotted a photographer taking pictures of the bridal party. The horse must have been a prop for the pictures. She was so distracted that she didn't realize Grammy E had walked up next to her.

"There's my other beautiful violinist!" Grammy E said. "I just talked with Jenny."

"Grammy E!!" Addy said, hugging her grandma, being careful not to knock Grammy E's flowered thermos of English tea out of her hand.

"When did you get here?" she asked.

"Just a little while ago. This place is gorgeous! Did you know that this ranch also provides equine therapy for students from the local schools?"

"What's equine therapy, Grammy E?" Addy asked.

"Equine therapy is a form of therapy that uses interactions between people and horses to promote healing and health in the person receiving the therapy," Grammy E said.

"So, kind of like counseling while you ride horses?" Addy asked.

"Well, sort of...you know how your Aunt Grace offers special music therapy sessions with counselor Sean at the school? It's kind of like that, but with activities involving the horses, rather than activities involving music," Grammy E said.

"Oh. I've never heard of that before," Addy said bending down to take in the sweet scent of a large bouquet of flowers sitting outside the tent. Grammy E bent down to do the same.

"Mmmm. They smell as good as they look. Oh, I also just got a sneak peek at the bride as I was

saying hello to her mother, and she looks exquisite!"
Grammy E said.

Chapter 10

Towards the end of Bach's "Arioso," the grooms-men filed in front of the chairs and the pastor nodded to Grace Notes. After the opening eight-note melodic phrase of Pachabel's "Kanon in D," the bridesmaids began their walk down the aisle. When it was time for the three-year-old flower girl to walk, the aisle remained empty.

There was a bit of whispering in the crowd of people in the chairs and then sudden laughter. Addy looked over at Jenny, Ty, and Shaun with a question-ing expression as they all continued to play. Moments later the flower girl appeared with a chocolate-smeared smile and a half-eaten chocolate bar in her hand. She clumsily dropped flower petals from the basket hung on her arm as she juggled taking nibbles of the chocolate bar and tossing chocolatey flower petals around.

Addy couldn't help but chuckle. Knowing her own sister's need for sugar bribery now and then, she guessed that the chocolate was what helped her complete the trek down the aisle.

Ty caught Addy, Jenny, and Shaun's eyes, and they finished out the phrase, nodding their heads and instruments in unison to the slowing rhythm. Ty then confidently launched into the grand introduction at a forte level for the approaching bride. They all joined in and their music accompanied Kara down the aisle and into her waiting groom's arms.

The ceremony was lovely, and after the pastor prayed a blessing over the newly married husband

and wife, they danced down the aisle together to Handel's "The Rejoicing," which lightened the mood and made everyone smile.

After all the rows of people were dismissed to the reception under the tent, Addy noticed Sam standing nearby listening to their music with a wide grin on his face.

"You all are amazing," he said. "I sure wish I could play an instrument like that."

Shaun said, "You could learn too!" as he finished playing the final notes of Marcello's "Psalm 19".

Shaun tucked his viola under his arm and laid his bow on his stand as he turned to talk with Sam.

"Have you ever tried to play an instrument?" Shaun asked.

"Nah. My dad has a banjo that my grandpa used to play, but I've never really tried to play it. We're pretty busy with the horses around here. I love hearing all the music at the weddings we host, but

I've never thought that maybe I could learn to play. You're the youngest musicians I've ever seen play at a wedding," Sam added.

"Do you like any of our instruments?" Ty asked.

"I really like the strong sounds of the instrument you're playing," Sam said.

"Ah, this is a cello. And there's actually a string instrument even bigger than this one called a bass that makes even deeper sounds," Ty said.

"I think I saw one of those at a rodeo we went to last month," Sam said. "There was a band that played, but I didn't see that they used a stick like you're using."

"Oh, I bet they were plucking the strings like this," Ty said, plucking out a riff on a low string of his cello.

"Yeah, that's what he was doing," Sam said.

"So sometimes string players pluck the strings

with their fingers like this. It's called pizzicato. And sometimes string players use a bow like this," Ty said, holding up his bow.

"I think it would be really cool to play the bass," Sam said.

"Well, I think it would be really cool to ride horses like you do," Jenny said.

Sam grinned. "Oh yeah? Do you all live around here?"

"We live down in Tigothee Falls, but we will be in Aspen until tomorrow night," Addy said.

"If y'all are free tomorrow, y'all should come riding with us," Sam said. "Horses can take you to places and views you can't get to on your own."

"That's really kind of you to offer, Sam," Shaun said.

"Are you sure your parents wouldn't mind?" Ty asked.

"Oh no. They love meeting new people. Let

me talk to them and I'll have them talk to your parents," Sam said.

Sure enough, Sam's mom came over to their table towards the end of the reception and asked Mrs. Gilman and Mrs. Belsky if they would like to join their family for a ride the next day. They talked through details and planned to meet after lunch.

Chapter 11

"I haven't ridden a horse in ten years," Grammy E said, as Sam's mom helped her onto a light gray horse that pawed at the ground once she was in the saddle.

Sam and his dad helped the rest of the group mount their horses and gave them some basic instructions.

They were soon riding along a dirt path that skirted up against a thick forest at the base of the mountains.

"How do we know these horses aren't going to just take off up into the mountains with us on them?" Addy suddenly asked, the anxiety in her voice obvious.

"The horses you are riding have all been trained to stay on the trail we are riding today, so you don't need to worry about getting lost," Mrs. Reed, Sam's mother told her, smiling reassuringly.

Addy took a deep breath and exhaled audibly.

"Remember, Addy, Fear not..." Grammy E said, winking at Addy. Grammy E had taught Addy to say the verse Isaiah 41:10 when she was feeling worried.

"And if it makes you feel any better, Clancy there has lived on the ranch here his whole life and he is probably our most laid back horse in the group. Notice that you're in the back with me. That's where Clancy likes to stay. He isn't in any hurry," Mrs. Reed continued, winking at Addy.

Addy smiled, whispered the verse quietly, and

relaxed into her saddle for the ride.

Mr. Reed was leading the group while Sam stayed in the middle of the group with his horse, Rocket. Before long they were crossing a small stream. All the horses slowed their gaits and stepped slowly across, as if they knew how to tiptoe through the rocky path below the water.

Grammy E's horse was in front of Addy a few steps from the shore when her horse mis-stepped and lunged forward suddenly. Before she knew what had happened, Grammy E had slid forward down the horse's neck like a playground slide and crashed into the stream.

"Grammy E!! Are you okay?" Addy yelled.

Mrs. Reed jumped off of her horse next to Addy and tugged it forward by the reins until she reached Grammy E.

"Are you alright?" Mrs. Reed asked, helping Grammy E up.

"Well, other than some lost pride and now soaked trousers, I guess I'm just fine," Grammy E said, walking through the foot-deep water with Mrs. Reed the final few steps to shore.

Sam had heard the splash and turned around. He jumped off of Rocket and grabbed the reins of Grammy E's horse from the stream as Addy's horse tromped back to shore.

Grammy E was giggling by the time Addy reached her. "Well, now I can tell people I've been bucked off a horse," she said with an ornery glint in her eye.

Addy just shook her head. Her Grammy E was one tough tea biscuit.

"Hey, Sam. Why don't you and Rocket head back to the ranch real quick for a blanket for Grammy E," Mrs. Reed said. "Would that be helpful?" she asked, turning to Grammy E.

"Oh sure, if it's not too much trouble. I'm not

missing the rest of this ride!" Grammy E said, lifting her soaked leg up to get back in the saddle.

"And grab the salve ointment for Smokey. It looks like he cut his shin a bit on something in the stream. It's just a small scrape and he'll be fine to keep riding, but I'd like to put something on it."

"Sure thing, Mom," Sam said.

"We'll meet you up at the vista," Mrs. Reed said.

With that, Sam galloped off with Rocket back across the stream and disappeared through the woods.

"You let that boy go by himself?" Grammy E asked curiously.

"These woods are Sam's back yard. He has a radio in the saddle if he gets in trouble, but he and Rocket will be fine—and speedy. Just you wait," Mrs. Reed said, winking.

Chapter 12

The riders began climbing the mountain on a switchback trail, stopping for a water and snack break at a large vista overlooking the ranch below. Sure enough, shortly after they arrived, they heard galloping hooves on the trail behind them slowing to a trot—and Sam and Rocket appeared, a blanket draped across the saddle and a can of ointment in his shirt pocket.

"How did you do that?" Shaun asked Sam, looking amazed.

"Well, we don't call him Rocket for nothing!" Sam said, laughing and patting his horse on the neck. Rocket shook his head and snorted as if in agreement. Shaun laughed.

The group dismounted and the Reeds helped them tie their horses to a few posts near an overlook.

"Hey, check this out!" Sam said a few moments later, pulling a pair of binoculars from his face and handing them to Ty.

"Oh, not another one!" Ty exclaimed.

"Wait, are there two?" Sam asked, grabbing them back to look.

"No, it's just that—" Ty began as Mr. Reed jogged over.

"Alright eagle eyes, what did you spot?" Mr. Reed asked, looking at Sam in anticipation.

"Dad, you know how you've been wondering what's been getting into your feed bin out in the second barn?" Sam asked.

Mr. Reed grabbed the binoculars from Sam.

"That ornery little bear cub!!" Mr. Reed suddenly exclaimed.

"I knew it was a bear!" Sam said.

"And we need to check that electric fence tonight because part of it must not be working properly," Mr. Reed commented.

"Agreed. We do NOT need bears near the livestock," Mrs. Reed said.

Mr. Reed made a phone call to his ranch hand while everyone took turns watching through the binoculars. A wide black truck soon pulled up to the barn, which startled the bear and sent him back across the open field and into the mountain forests.

"Maybe we just attract bears," Jenny suggested, her eyes wide and looking around in concern.

"Oh, don't worry while you're riding. We are quite a cacophonous crew. No bear is going to want to take on all of us at once," Mr. Reed said, grinning.

Jenny, Addy, Shaun and Ty shared their bear-thief story and had the Reeds laughing as they trotted back to the horse barn.

Chapter 13

When they arrived back at the barn, Sam called out to a girl standing on the second rung of the wooden fence of the barn lot and affectionately petting the nose of a white horse.

"Hi, Sara!"

"Hey, Sam! Sounds like you have company," Sara replied, turning toward them but not making eye contact with them.

"I sure do. Friends, I would like to introduce you to one of my favorite people around—Miss Sara Lane," Sam said.

"Hi, Sara! It's nice to meet you," Jenny said,

sliding down from her horse. "I'm Jenny."

"And I'm Addy," Addy said, following Jenny's lead.

The rest of the group introduced themselves.

"Wait a minute," Shaun said, looking at Sara. "Are you from around here or have you ever been to Tigothee Falls? You look familiar."

"Oh, you probably saw my fundraising boxes around town," Sara said, laughing.

"When I was nine years old, I began losing my eyesight. Within the year, I was diagnosed with a rare degenerative disorder that made me lose my ability to see. As you can imagine, it was a rough year. Anyways, I started coming here to Sunset Ranch, and, as I worked with the horses, I gained confidence that I could live without full use of my sight. It's been two years, and while I've learned to navigate pretty well without my vision, I've realized how helpful it would be to have a service dog.

"I've seen a few those dogs. They're amazing," Addy said.

"My parents and I started researching and discovered it would cost $17,000 to get one," Sara continued. "We have been raising funds and those boxes at the restaurants and lodges in town have brought in a lot of money towards our goal in the last year. In fact, we're now only $500 short of our goal!"

"Sara, that's wonderful!" Sam said. "I knew you thought you were close to your goal last week when you were here."

"I'm so excited!" Sara said. "My parents and I have been in contact with the organization that raises and trains the dogs. I can't wait to begin the training process once we have all the funds secured."

The group helped return their horses to their stalls and thanked the Reeds again for the ride.

"Well, Grace Notes, I sure do hope we get to

meet again some day!" Sam said, waving to them as they turned to go.

"The feeling is mutual, Sam!" Shaun said, speaking for all of them. "And good luck with that guide dog, Sara."

"Thanks!" Sara said, smiling and waving.

The group parted ways with Grammy E at Sunset Ranch as they drove separate vehicles. Grammy E was staying in Aspen for the evening for one final visit with her friend Mrs. Thompson.

Chapter 14

"Now that was a weekend!" Mrs. Gilman said as they began their drive home from Aspen that evening.

"It sure was. And what a treat to get to ride horses today! I had no idea we would get to do that," Mrs. Belsky said.

"My favorite part was riding Susie," Gabby said, referring to the pony she rode at Sunset Ranch.

"I loved the views. I felt like we were so far from everything. It was as if we were entering a storybook or something," Addy said.

"I loved crossing the streams," said Jenny.

"I liked getting to meet Sam and Sara," Shaun said.

"Yeah. I keep thinking about Sara and her positive outlook on life," Ty said. "I'm so thankful for my sight…I can't imagine losing it."

"Yeah. Me either," Shaun said.

Mrs. Gilman and Mrs. Belsky began talking to each other and weren't really paying attention to the conversation that continued in the back of the vehicle.

"Hey, do you all think…" Addy wondered aloud, in a lowered voice.

"I knew I wasn't the only one thinking what you're thinking," Ty said, beginning to smile.

"Wait, what?" Jenny asked, not quite catching where their thoughts were going.

"Come on, Jenny, the GDC?" Shaun said with questioning eyebrows.

There was a pause and then Jenny exclaimed, "Ahh, yes - of course! The Good Deed Crew…"

"If we each give a little bit, we could totally make her guide dog dream a reality even this week," Shaun whispered.

"I'll see if I can get the correct address to send the money to," Addy said. "I took an information card that was next to the fundraising box at the hotel. I think that there was a fundraising website set up in Sara's name."

"Shaun and I can mail out the money when we go to the post office tomorrow," Ty offered.

Shaun nodded.

"Guess we'll have to wait on those glasses, brother. I mean, who needs expensive biking glasses when we can give someone a bit of their sight back through a guide dog?" Shaun said, shrugging his shoulders.

Ty smiled in return.

Chapter 15

Nothing but a flowered plate of blueberry muffin crumbs remained. Grammy E picked up the plate from the table and smiled. She loved having Grace Notes practice in her home. It was a couple of weeks after the Aspen adventure and they were practicing for yet another summer wedding.

"Hey there kids. Your music sounds wonderful as always," Grammy E said, walking into her living room.

"Do you all remember Mrs. Thompson?"

"Yeah," Shaun replied.

"I was on the phone with her last night and she was filling me in on the latest news in Aspen."

Addy and Jenny glanced at one another.

"Do you remember that sweet girl we met at Sunset Ranch? Sara was her name, I believe. Anyways, she received a sizeable anonymous donation the week after we left that allowed her to finally receive her guide dog."

"Oh, that's wonderful, Grammy E," Ty said, not missing a beat.

"Yeah, that's so great," Addy said.

Shaun and Jenny nodded their agreement.

"Now who could have done such an act of kindness?" Grammy E asked, her eyebrows raised. She paused and squinted at the group, her suspicion written clearly across her face.

The group looked at one another, stifled smiles and shuffled their sheet music on the stands a bit.

"Let's take it from the top, crew…uh…er…I mean…Grace Notes," Jenny said.

Grammy E just turned and walked out of the room shaking her head, her shoulders moving up and down to her audible laughter and saying, "Bless you, kids, bless you."

"Way to keep it top secret, crew. Remember, humility is our code of honor," Ty whispered slightly above the music as they played.

When pride comes, then comes disgrace, but with humility comes wisdom.

Proverbs 11:2

Grammy E's Blueberry Pie

Ingredients:

pastry for 2-crust, 9-inch pie
3/4 c. sugar
4 T. cornstarch
1/4 tsp. ground cinnamon
pinch of salt

5 c. fresh blueberries
1 T. butter
1 egg whisked with a dash of milk
sugar for sprinkling

Directions:

Preheat oven to 375°. Place single piecrust in pie plate. Mix sugar, cornstarch, cinnamon and salt. Carefully mix in blueberries. Pour into unbaked pie crust. Slice small pieces of butter over blueberry mixture. Place pie crust on top and seal around edge.

Slice a pretty design on top of the pie and brush it with egg/milk. Sprinkle with sugar and bake at 375° for 50 minutes or until lightly browned on top. Cool to set. Share warm with vanilla ice cream and enjoy!

💜 "There's nothing like sharing a warm baked pie to warm hearts." Grammy E

Good Deed Crew Memory Verse

"Fear not for I am with thee."

Isaiah 41:10

GRACE NOTES

Join Grace Notes for their next adventure:

The Good Deed Crew
and the Art of Giving

It's summer and Addy has some questions after Grace Notes plays music for the "Art in the Park" event. Will her answers lead The Good Deed Crew to its next act of kindness?

Enjoy a sneak preview of the first chapter NOW!

Chapter 1

"Hello up there! Do you need a drink of lemonade?" Mrs. Gilman asked.

Addy finished reading a sentence of *The Secret Garden* and peered down through the green leaves of the tree she was sitting in to see her mom standing below. She was holding a light blue thermos of lemonade and some fresh purple grapes in a bowl.

"Sure. Send them up," Addy said, grinning and lowering a basket on a pulley rope down to the ground.

Mrs. Gilman filled the basket and Addy smiled when she retrieved her snack moments later, and read the note from her mom. She loved the way her mom tucked in sweet ways of loving her throughout her everyday moments. She prayed she could do the same for her kids one day.

"I love you too, Mom!" Addy called to her mom who was already stepping onto the back porch. Her smiling mom turned around and waved.

It was the middle of August and Addy was enjoying her final schedule-free summer days before they started their homeschool work again the following week. She was determined to get through her summer reading list of "fun" books she had compiled in June. She was close. After a few sips of her fresh lemonade and a handful of grapes, she was soon whisked back into the garden with Mary and Dickon.

An hour later it was Jenny's voice that pulled

her eyes from the page.

"Addy! Aren't you coming down? Practice is in ten minutes!" Jenny called up to her.

"Ah!! I totally forgot we were practicing to-day!" Addy said, snapping the book closed and feeling her body ache from sitting in the same position for so long, lost in secret worlds of ink.

"I'm on my way. Are Shaun and Ty here yet?"

Addy dropped the remains of her snack and her book into the basket and lowered it to the ground next to Jenny.

"Nope. Your mom didn't remember either and I kind of surprised her. She didn't seem to mind though," Jenny said.

"Not being on our regular weekly schedule really throws me off in the summer. I forget what day it is sometimes," Addy said, carefully climbing down through the branches of her favorite reading tree.

She and Jenny went into the house and began setting up the front room with stands, and getting their instruments out.

"Hello-o-o?" Ty sang out, through the front screen door.

"Come on in!" Addy called, her back turned to them as she pulled her violin out.

"Hi there!" Shaun said, following Ty into the room.

"I was just at Miss Carmen's helping her organize some supplies for this weekend. I kind of wish I was going to be a participant in the Art Fair. Seriously, Gabby needs to come. There are going to be so many great projects for kids to do!" Shaun said.

Miss Carmen, the art teacher at their co-op, had asked Grace Notes to provide music for the Art in the Park event that weekend for kids in the community. There were about twenty different artists in the area providing hands-on activities for kids to create and take home with them in hopes of inspiring future artists.

"Oh, she'll be there. Mom is hosting a booth, you know," Addy said.

"Oh yeah, I saw her name on the list of artists. I just wasn't sure if Gabby was planning to come or stay with Grammy E. Like I said, we might have to take a little break to make a few things. This is only the second year of the fair, but it sounds like it is going to be amazing," Shaun said.

Jenny sat at the Steinway grand piano in Addy's front room and squeezed her violin between her chin and shoulder as she played an A on the piano with her left hand and pulled her bow across her instrument with her right hand. She adjusted the tuning peg on her violin until the pitch of the notes sounded the same. She then tuned the other strings and finished by playing an A for the rest of the group.

"'Scuse us! Royalty coming through," Addy's five-year-old sister Gabby announced.

She had appeared from the back of the house carrying her white Bischon dog. Princess Petunia, the aformentioned royal pup, was wearing a tiny sequined gold and pink cape and Gabby was holding a small doll-sized crown on her head. The dog was tolerating it surprisingly well. She put Petunia down to go out the door and then peered out the window waiting for the royal pup to do her business.

"I like her style, Gabs," Jenny said approvingly.

"Thanks. She has impectable taste," Gabby said, very seriously.

"You mean impeccable, Gabby, but good word!" Addy said, laughing.

Gabby nodded in agreement, then continued her watch out the window.

Jenny turned back to the musicians in the room.

"I know we pretty much have our playlist to-gether for the weekend, but we have to try out this new arrangement of Haydn's "Surprise Symphony," Jenny said. She pulled a folder of music from her patchwork shimmery hand-quilted shoulder bag.

Ty looked it over and picked out a few mea-sures on his cello. Shaun and Addy did the same, each in their own world for a few minutes. When they finished individually looking over their parts, they looked at one another's music and conferred.

"Looks good to me," Shaun said.

"I agree. I like that the surprise chord gets sort of passed around to each of us with this version," Ty commented.

"Yeah, let's try it out and see how it goes," Addy suggested.

They were almost to the end of the piece when there was a loud crash outside that literally shook the house. Gabby screamed.

About the Author:

Kendra Parks grew up reading books up in trees and playing her own violin in a traveling string quartet. She has a college degree in Communications-Journalism and has taught violin lessons and played music in countless venues. Her heart in writing Grace Notes is to create fun stories centered around her love of music with moments of real-life faith included rather than edited out. She longs to create characters kids can identify with and emulate, knowing that God has amazing plans for their lives and that they can do great things in a humble way, regardless of their young age. She currently lives, creates and writes on the edge of a magical forest with her best friend/husband who is also a writer, four brilliant dreamers, and their fluffy tail-wagging pup.

Other books by Kendra Parks:

Grace Notes Series

Book #1

Book #2

Book #3

Book #4

Find out about our upcoming writing projects at:

www.ParksWrites.com

Made in the USA
Monee, IL
21 February 2022

91594978R00059